written by Judith Stamper illustrated by Craig Spearing

SCHOLASTIC INC.
New York Toronto London Auckland Sydney
Mexico City New Delhi Hong Kong Buenos Aires

Developed by Kirchoff/Wohlberg, Inc., in cooperation with Scholastic Inc.

 Published by Scholastic Inc. Printed in the U.S.A.
ISBN 0-439-35113-8

15 16 17 18 19 20 40 15 14 13 12 11 10

May 18, 1849

Dear Ma, Sarah, Jeb, and Smiley,

California is only ten days away!

I'm sitting on a rock and writing you this letter. The wagon train had to stop because one wagon broke down. We'll get moving again soon.

So far, the trip has been hard. Some people ran out of food and had to return home. Others got sick. Pa and I have been lucky so far.

Tomorrow we start across the desert. It's California or bust!

It seems so long since I saw you all. Sarah, do you still want to be a teacher? Jeb, are you still growing? Ma, I miss your cooking!

Pet Smiley for me. Next time you see us, Pa and I will be rich. We'll all be rich!

Your loving son and brother,

Luke

June 1, 1849

Dear Ma, Sarah, Jeb, and Smiley,

Pa and I got to San Francisco last night. People are here from all over the world. They all want to be in the Gold Rush.

The harbor here is crowded with boats. All the sailors went off to find gold. Now there is no one to sail the ships home!

Everyone calls us greenhorns because we're new here. We have a lot of things to get used to.

This morning Pa and I went to a store. We bought a new kind of pants. They're called Levis. A man named Levi Strauss made them.

The pants are for hardworking folk. They are made of strong cloth. You can load the pockets and they still won't tear!

Tomorrow we go up to Sacramento.

Your son and brother,

Luke

June 26, 1849

Dear Ma, Sarah, Jeb, and Smiley,

I'm writing to you by campfire. Pa and I are sleeping outside tonight. We traveled farther north into the hills today. We unloaded our tools and made camp.

We're on our way to Grizzly Flat. That's a place where they've found gold.

Yesterday, we bought tools in Sacramento. We got only things we really needed :

- a shovel to dig up dirt and sand
- a pick to break up pieces of rock
- a pan to remove the gold from the dirt

We also bought a tent and more food. Pa is asleep right now, but I'm too excited to sleep.

Your son and brother,

Luke

July 13, 1849

Dear Ma, Sarah, Jeb, and Smiley,

Pa and I have staked our claim. Pa and I found a place that was undiscovered. We hammered a stake in the ground.

We called it "Smiley's Claim." Some other miners asked us who Smiley is. They said he's going to be one rich dog!

Pa and I are looking for placer gold. That is gold that remains in dry river beds.

Pa and I started panning for gold this morning. Pa digs up a scoop of dirt and gravel. He puts it in the pan. I lower the pan into the stream, and then I slowly pour off the water. If there's gold, it'll be left in the bottom of the pan.

Your tired son and brother,

Luke

September 6, 1849

Dear Ma, Sarah, Jeb, and Smiley,

Whoopee! Pa and I found gold today!

I had been panning all morning. Then all of a sudden, I saw it. The gold was uncovered at the bottom of my pan.

Real quick, Pa dug up more dirt from the same place. We saw two more nuggets. Pa and I yelled so loud that other miners came running. They said it was gold all right.

Pa and I found four more nuggets. It looks like "Smiley's Claim" is a good one.

Tonight we're going to sleep with the gold under our pillows. Tomorrow we will take it into Sacramento. Soon, Pa and I will be sending money home.

I'm putting out the lantern. I just want to sleep now and dream about gold.

Your tired son and brother,

Luke

September 7, 1849

Dear Ma, Sarah, Jeb, and Smiley,

Sacramento is a boom town! Everything about it has boomed—people, buildings, stores, and streets. The streets are full of people, horses, and wagons, too.

Pa and I went to the office to have our gold nuggets weighed. We got $60 for them. We also went to register our claim.

Sometimes people start mining on land that has been claimed by somebody else. Now Pa has proof that the spot is ours.

Pa and I went to celebrate. We got a real home-cooked meal. Then we went to a store. We replaced our worn-out blankets. We could have stayed longer, but Pa wanted to get back to the claim. It's a good thing we did, too!

Two miners were pulling up our stake! They were claim *jumpers*! I guess they had heard about the gold we found.

Pa told them to drop our stake. One of the men reached in his pocket. I got really scared, but he *just* pulled out a map. He acted like he was lost. Then they both left.

Pa and I reclaimed our land. My knees shook for hours, though.

Your son and brother,
Luke

October 16, 1849

Dear Ma, Sarah, Jeb, and Smiley,

I'm sorry you have not heard from me in so long. Pa fell sick last week. I took care of him and he's better now.

The weather has turned cold. At night, the wind whips around our tent. We hope the winter passes quickly.

We have some good news. Pa said I should write you about it.

Three weeks ago, we struck it rich! Pa and I were digging along the stream. Then, chunks of gold started falling down!

Right away, Pa took the gold into Sacramento to the bank. We're going to stay until next summer. Then we're coming home.

I'm glad about that. I've learned one thing about gold. It can't take the place of people you love.

Your loving son and brother,

Luke